Alone in the Night

Alone in the Night

Holly Webb

Illustrated by Sophy Williams

SCHOLASTIC INC.

New York Toronto London Auckland
Sydney Mexico City New Delhi Hong Kong

For Tom

ISBN 978-0-545-32576-9

All rights reserved. Published by Scholastic Inc., 557 Broadway, New York, NY 10012.
SCHOLASTIC and associated logos are trademarks and/or registered trademarks of Scholastic Inc. Lexile is a registered trademark of MetaMetrics, Inc.

12 11 10 9 8 7 6 5 4 3 2 1   11 12 13 14 15 16/0

Printed in the U.S.A.   40
First Scholastic printing, November 2011

Chapter One

"Jasmine! Hurry up! You're going to be late for school!" Jasmine's mom glanced at her watch—and then at all the other children heading to school, streaming past the end of their road.

Jasmine looked up. "But I was just saying hello to Tiger, Mom!" The marmalade tabby cat sitting on the wall ducked his head so Jasmine could rub his ears. Then he stood up and leaned over to bump the side of his head against her chin. Jasmine had read lots of books about cats and knew that he wasn't just being cute. He was rubbing his scent glands on her. It was pretty cute, too, though. All the cats in the neighborhood loved Jasmine—which is why it always took her so long to get to school.

"Jasmine, we left the house ten minutes ago and we haven't even gotten past next door!" Her mom sighed. "You're going to be *late*."

"Sorry, Mom." Jasmine smiled at her apologetically. "Let's run!"

She was just picking up her school-bag when she stopped again. "Oh, Mom, look! In the house next door's window!"

She pointed across the yard.

"Oh, a kitten."

"Mom! An *adorable* kitten! I haven't seen her before. Did you know the new people next door had a kitten?"

The kitten was tiny, perched right in the middle of the big windowsill, which made her look even tinier. Jasmine could just about make out her beautiful striped brown tabby markings.

"No, I didn't," Mom said, leading her away. Jasmine walked backward, still staring at the kitten, who stared back. "We haven't really said any more than a quick hello to them while they were unpacking."

"Poor little kitten. They must have left her all alone while they went to work," Jasmine said sadly.

"Oh, Jasmine! Cats don't mind being on their own." Her mom laughed. "Besides, how do you even know that kitten's a she? It could be a boy."

"She just looked like a she," Jasmine said. "And cats do get lonely, Mom, especially when they're babies."

"I'm sure they'll play with her when they get home," Mom comforted her. "Now run!"

Jasmine turned out to be right—the kitten was a girl. Her mom invited Helen, the new neighbor next door, over for coffee, and found out all about the beautiful cat.

"She's named Star," Jasmine told her best friend, Lara, as they walked home from school together. "She's got such cute tabby stripes. She's really pretty." Jasmine sighed. "She looks exactly like my dream cat—you know, the one I'd really like to have for my own someday."

"Oh, you're so lucky that she's just next door," Lara said enviously. "She might even come into your yard! Do you know how old she is?"

"Nearly three months," Jasmine said. "She was given to the neighbors by a friend whose cat had kittens. They were worried she might be upset by the move, but she doesn't mind. Except she's desperate to go out!"

"Can't they let her out?" Lara asked.

"Not until she's gotten all of her vaccinations, which will be a few weeks," Jasmine explained. "See you tomorrow!"

she called as they got to her gate.

Over the next few weeks, Jasmine watched for Star every time she walked past the house next door, and always waved hello. Sometimes, if the little cat was sitting on the windowsill, she would stand up on her back legs and scrabble hopefully at the glass with her paws, as though she wanted to slip through and come out for Jasmine to pet her. Jasmine wished she could, too.

Star finished washing herself and looked thoughtfully around the yard. She still wasn't very used to being outside. In fact, today was the first day that her owners had left her in the house with the cat flap unlocked. She'd been allowed out all on her own a few times over the weekend, and they'd put out big bowls of cat treats to make sure she came back. Of course she did! She loved her house, and her basket, and her food bowls, and her people. Exploring was fun, too, that was all.

She headed to the end of the yard. The brambles there were fascinating, full of nests and tunnels and hidey-holes. When she'd finally finished investigating and wriggled out again, her eyes were sparkling with excitement. She licked the fur around her mouth thoughtfully, trying to get rid of the strange taste of beetle. Beetles looked delicious, like walking cat treats, but they didn't taste good.

Star sat down in the middle of the lawn, closing her eyes for a moment and feeling the warm autumn sunshine on her fur. Then she went and rolled around in a pile of dried leaves. When she got bored of that game, she stretched out her front paws and her back paws, and looked for something to do next. There was a snail moving very slowly along a leaf right next to her, and she watched it for a little while, but she'd learned from the beetle, and didn't try to eat it.

That was when she spotted the gap under the fence. Star didn't really know what the fence was. She didn't quite understand that there was a whole new yard on the other side of it. But she knew that the little hole looked interesting.

The gap wasn't very big, and she had to scratch a little at the ground underneath to get through. Star still had little, soft indoor kitten paws, with apricot pink pads, and digging her way under the fence rubbed off a little of their newness. It felt good.

She emerged in the yard next door and gave herself a quick bath. Then she looked around with interest.

Suddenly, she caught sight of Jasmine. Her eyes widened—Jasmine had been so quiet, Star had thought she was alone. But she didn't dive back under the fence. Star recognized the girl—she was the friendly one who always waved when she walked past the house.

It was a long weekend off from school. Jasmine was in the yard putting out leftover toast crusts from breakfast for the birds when she caught a little grayish-brown flash in the corner of her eye. She turned her head slowly, hoping to see what sort of bird it was. But it wasn't a sparrow hopping around in the bushes. It was a cat.

Not just any cat—*the* cat. It was little Star, from next door.

She was squeezing herself under the fence, wriggling and scrabbling, with such a determined expression on her face that Jasmine had to bite her lip to stop herself from giggling—she didn't want to scare Star away.

The kitten finally popped out from under the fence like she'd been pushed, and twitched her tail. Then she sat down to bathe herself, brushing her paw thoroughly around her ears in case she'd gotten them dirty fighting her way through.

Jasmine perched on the yard bench and watched her, not even wanting to breathe too deeply in case she frightened the tiny creature. She'd been hoping to meet Star in person for so long, and the kitten was only a few yards away.

Now Star had obviously seen her. She stood up daintily and padded over to Jasmine. No one had pet her since Helen and Andy left for work, and even though exploring was fun, she wanted someone to fuss over her. She stopped a little way away, just far enough to make a run for it if Jasmine turned out not to be friendly, and gave a hopeful little meow.

Jasmine reached out her hand slowly. She couldn't believe Star had come this close—she'd thought that such a little kitten would be too nervous. She could almost touch Star's nose, but she didn't. She just held her fingers out and whispered, "Here, kitty, hello, Star . . ."

Star's ears pricked slightly. The girl knew her name! That had to be good.

She pranced a few steps closer and rubbed her head affectionately against Jasmine's leg.

Jasmine laughed and began to scratch Star's ears, and Star made a big leap and sprang onto the bench next to her, then climbed into her lap. There Star gave a contented little sigh and closed her eyes, massaging Jasmine's jeans with her little needle-sharp claws. Good. Some decent petting.

Jasmine smiled down at her, wishing she had a beautiful kitten of her very own. It was such a pity her mom and dad weren't really pet people. But could wonderful little Star help convince them?

From then on, Jasmine always looked out for Star in the yard, and Star soon figured out what time Jasmine got home from school. If she was bored or wanted someone to play with, she would wriggle under the fence—she'd made the hole much bigger by now—and jump from the bench onto the kitchen windowsill. Then she would meow plaintively for Jasmine to come out and see her.

Jasmine's mom thought it was funny at first, but then she started to worry. What if the next-door neighbors minded that Jasmine spent so much time fussing over their kitten?

One day the kitchen window was open—Jasmine's mom had been cooking chili for dinner and wanted to air out the room. When Jasmine came into the kitchen, she saw Star nosing curiously around the gap, obviously wondering if she was allowed to step in through the window.

Jasmine didn't even think. She just held out her hand and called gently to Star, tempting her in. She couldn't imagine anything nicer than cuddling Star in her own kitchen. Unless it was in her bedroom, of course. . . .

Jasmine's mom was horrified when she came upstairs to see how Jasmine was doing with her homework. "Jasmine! What's that cat doing in here?" she cried.

Star gave a nervous little squeak and disappeared off Jasmine's lap to under the desk.

Jasmine glared at her mom and crouched down to try and coax Star out. "You scared her!"

"She scared me!" her mom retorted. "She's not supposed to be in our house, Jasmine—she lives next door!"

"I bet they wouldn't mind," Jasmine muttered. She knew she shouldn't really have let Star in, but she'd looked so lonely, meowing on the windowsill. "They don't get home till later, Mom; she just wanted to cuddle!"

"Jasmine, she's not ours. She'll end up getting confused about where she lives—she's still young. Put her out!" her mom said firmly. And Jasmine had to gather Star up and take her back downstairs.

"Sorry, Star!" Jasmine murmured as she slipped the kitten out the back door. Her mom was watching, her arms folded sternly, and Jasmine knew she'd be pushing her luck if she went outside, too. But it was getting dark and had started to rain. She felt so guilty putting Star out in the cold and wet.

Star watched the door close, looking up at it sadly. Why hadn't Jasmine's mother wanted her there? She didn't understand. She shook her whiskers, feeling confused, then slunk across the yard, under the fence, and back through her cat flap.

Chapter Two

After Mom had made her take Star outside, Jasmine didn't risk letting her in the house again, no matter how much she wanted to. For the next few weeks, she played with Star in the yard instead, even though it was November and freezing cold. Star's pretty furry coat kept her a lot warmer than Jasmine's jacket, but she didn't want to miss out on playing with the kitten.

"Jasmine! Come on in, it's dinner-time!" Jasmine's mom called from the back door.

Jasmine picked up Star and put her gently on top of the fence—she liked jumping onto it now that she was bigger, instead of scrabbling through underneath. "Bye, Star! See you tomorrow," Jasmine murmured, petting the little cat's nose. Star was in that funny stage now where she was half-kitten, half-cat, and all legs.

Her mom was still looking out the back door. "Aren't you frozen?" she said. "Look, your hands are bright red—where are your gloves?"

Jasmine wiggled her fingers, which had started to feel numb. "I was petting

Star—you can't pet a cat with gloves on, Mom."

Her mom shook her head, smiling. "You and that cat."

Star jumped lightly down from the fence and trotted back to her cat flap. She was very cold and she wanted to go inside. But when she nudged her cat flap with her nose, it didn't open. Star butted it harder, but she only hurt her nose. She meowed fiercely. Then she tried scratching at the cat flap, but that didn't work, either. The flap was stuck, and it wouldn't budge.

Star meowed again, louder this time, hoping her owners would hear. But no one came. Miserably, she crept away and hid under a bush close to the door, waiting for the house lights to go on to show that her owners were home.

It seemed as though she would have to wait forever, while the yard grew darker and darker and colder. Even her tail ached with the cold. It was too chilly to sleep, and she was so hungry. She got up and went to stare sadly through the cat flap at her food bowl. Usually her owners would be home by now, she was sure. Where were they? Star didn't like being on her own. She liked people and being petted. She looked back across the dark yard to Jasmine's house. If only she could go inside. It would be so nice and warm in there.

Suddenly, the fur on her back rose up as she sensed that another cat was in her yard, and not one she liked. She'd met quite a few other cats over the last few weeks. Some had been friendly, and some had warned her away. She jumped around, whiskers bristling, and saw an enormous dark shape creeping toward her. A dark shape that *hissed*.

Star squeaked with fright and backed up against the wall, darting a quick, desperate glance at her cat flap. But it was still shut tight.

The black cat padded closer and hissed again, and then swiped at her with one huge dark paw, sending her skidding away.

Star skittered across the yard and dived for the hole under the fence. Frantically, she squeezed her way through, even though it was almost too tight, and shot out into Jasmine's yard. At least the hole was too small for that huge black cat to follow her. Star ran over to Jasmine's back door and let out a panicky howl, hoping Jasmine would come and rescue her.

She'd been right. The hole was too small for the black cat. But she could hear him scrambling up the fence. . . .

Jasmine was asleep, dreaming of a horrible spelling test, when her teacher suddenly turned into a meowing cat. She wriggled and turned over, muttering in her sleep. But the meowing didn't stop, and eventually she woke up, blinking worriedly into the darkness. That was Star!

Jasmine hopped out of bed and threw on her robe. She was leaning over the top of the stairs when her dad came out of the living room.

"Oh, did they wake you, Jasmine?

Don't be scared; it's just some cats fighting outside. I'm going to chase them away."

Jasmine shook her head anxiously, and ran down the stairs toward him. "No, Dad, don't! That sounds like Star, the kitten from next door. I'm sure she's not fighting. She's really scared, I can tell."

Her dad sighed. "Your mom said you'd fallen in love with that cat. Come on, let's see what's going on."

He opened the back door, and there on the step, shivering, was a tiny little tabby cat, her fur all up on end and her tail looking like a feather duster. Lurking a couple of yards away, its eyes shining green in the light from the kitchen, was the biggest black cat

Jasmine had ever seen.

"Oh! It's Sam, from down the road," she said. "He's always fighting. He's only got half an ear, and Mrs. James has to take him to the vet about every other week. We can't let him fight with Star—he's so huge he'd just squash her!" Jasmine went out onto the step, not caring about her bare feet. "Shoo, Sam! Go home, bad cat!"

Sam backed off, but only a little bit. Star gave a miserable little meow, and Jasmine picked her up gently. "Dad, can we please bring her inside? I know the Murrays wouldn't mind, not if she was going to get hurt."

Her dad sighed and looked over at her mom, who'd come into the kitchen to see what was happening.

"Why can't she go home?" Mom asked, sounding reluctant. "Doesn't she have a cat flap?"

Jasmine shrugged. "Maybe she's too scared to get past Sam?"

"I'll run next door and see if the

Murrays are home. It didn't look like their lights were on, though." Dad went around to the front of the house.

Jasmine cuddled Star, feeling her heart racing inside her fragile body. She was still such a little cat.

Dad came back, shaking his head. "No, they're definitely out."

Jasmine's mom sighed. "Well, maybe we had better hold on to her. Just till Helen and Andy get home. They must have gone out for the evening."

Even though it was late, Jasmine's mom and dad let her stay downstairs with Star—it was a Friday evening, so there was no school the next day. And when Jasmine pointed out that Star probably hadn't had any dinner, Mom even found a can of tuna for her.

But it got later and later, and Jasmine couldn't stop yawning. Star was curled up fast asleep on her lap on the sofa, and Jasmine's mom shook her head, laughing.

"Go up to bed, Jasmine," she said. "And yes, you can take her with you, otherwise I'm sure she'll howl herself silly in the kitchen. We'll just have to take her back in the morning."

Jasmine looked up at her in delight. "Really?" She had been trying so hard not to yawn in case Mom sent her off to bed, but she'd never thought they'd let her take Star upstairs, not after what Mom had said the last time Star was there.

She stood up, draping sleepy little Star over her shoulder like a soft, furry scarf, and crept upstairs. She set Star down on her bed while she took off her robe, then snuggled carefully under the covers, trying not to disturb her.

Jasmine was just drifting off to sleep when she heard a quiet purring, right next to her ear, as Star burrowed down beside her. Jasmine smiled in her sleep and felt like purring, too.

The next morning Jasmine slept late after her exciting night, and it was nine o'clock when she and Star wandered downstairs. It had been so wonderful waking up and finding a cat curled up next to her!

Star sat on Jasmine's lap and sniffed hopefully at her toast. Jasmine smiled. "I think Star's hungry, Mom!"

Jasmine's mom looked at her worriedly. "I wonder what she usually has for breakfast. I don't want to make her sick with too much tuna."

Jasmine's dad looked over at them. "We ought to let the Murrays know where she is—they'll be worrying about her."

Jasmine sighed. She was enjoying pretending Star was hers, but it looked like the game wouldn't last long.

She was just finishing her toast when the doorbell rang, and her mom went to answer it. Jasmine could hear Mom chatting with someone, and then she came back in with Helen and Andy from next door.

Star gave a delighted little *prrp*, and jumped off Jasmine's lap, scampering over to Helen.

"That's not very grateful!" Helen laughed. "Jasmine, your mom says you saved Star from that great big black cat from down the road. Thank you for rescuing her." She shook her head. "She's been wandering off at night a lot lately. I know she's just getting bigger and braver, but I wish she wouldn't. Oh, well. Maybe she'll be a little less daring for a while after her scare."

Star trotted back over and rubbed her head up against Jasmine's leg. She was delighted to see her owners, but she did love Jasmine, too.

Helen gave Jasmine a thoughtful look, watching the way Star was snuggling against her.

While Jasmine said good-bye to Star, the Murrays went to talk to her mom and dad in the hallway.

"Jasmine, do you think you could do us a huge favor?" said Helen, as she came back into the kitchen and gathered up Star. "We're going away for three weeks over Christmas, and we haven't quite decided what to do with this little one. Star's such a friendly thing, we think she'd hate a boarding kennel, where no one would have much time to play with her." She paused. "Would you like to take care of her for us?"

Jasmine's eyes opened wide with delight and she looked hopefully at her mom and dad. To take care of Star, for three whole weeks! She couldn't imagine anything she'd like more.

Chapter Three

Jasmine was counting down the days until the Murrays went away. She and her mom went next door after school one night, so that the Murrays could go through everything Jasmine would need to know. They weren't going on vacation for another few days, but they wanted to get things organized in advance.

Star met them at the door, meowing with delight at the sight of Jasmine.

Helen laughed. "This was such a good idea! I was really worried about Star being miserable at a kennel. Come in."

They sat down at the kitchen table to look at a list that Helen had made of all the things she thought Jasmine would need to know, like the phone number of their vet, just in case.

Mom frowned. "I hope you can manage all this, Jasmine," she said, looking at the part about measuring out Star's special food so she didn't have too much.

"Don't worry, Mom, of course I can," Jasmine told her. "And I'll get up earlier so I can check in on Star before school and feed her."

But when they got home, Jasmine couldn't help worrying a little, too. Not about feeding Star and looking after her correctly—she was sure she could do that. No, she was worried about all the time Star would be on her own in the Murrays' house. She was a cat who loved attention and fuss—that's why she came into Jasmine's yard all the time. How would she feel about being alone every night? Now that it was December, it was getting really cold. Mom wasn't going to let Jasmine sit out in the yard with Star for very long if it started snowing!

Maybe Mom would let me bring her inside for some of the time? Jasmine wondered to herself. *I'm sure Helen and Andy wouldn't mind. . . . Oh!*

Jasmine smiled excitedly. She had just thought of a great idea.

What if she took care of Star at *her* house instead? It would be like having a cat of her very own!

Now all she had to do was persuade Mom and Dad. . . .

"But we don't want a cat in the house, Jasmine," Mom said. "It's all arranged. You'll feed Star next door."

Jasmine nodded. "I know, but it would be so much better if she was here. She's so friendly, Mom, and she'd hate being on her own all day. She'd be company for you while you're working." She looked at her mom hopefully. It wasn't just that she really wanted to have Star stay over—she was sure that Mom and Dad would fall in love with Star if they saw more of her. And if Jasmine could do a great job looking after Star and give her back to the Murrays as the world's best-cared-for cat, wouldn't her parents be tempted to let her have a cat of her own? Once they knew how nice it would be to have a cat in the house?

"Pets can be messy," Dad explained. "We don't have a cat flap, for one thing, so that would be a problem. . . ."

"But we could put a litter box in the corner of the kitchen," Jasmine suggested eagerly. "I bet the Murrays have one, and if not, I'll buy one with my allowance."

Mom smiled. "I thought you were saving up for my Christmas present!"

Jasmine grinned at her. "Oh, I bought your present a long time ago, when you let me go Christmas shopping with Lara. Please, Mom," she added. "It's only for three weeks. I promise you won't have to do anything—I'll take care of her all by myself. I'll even do the vacuuming, in case Star sheds hair on the carpet. Oh, pleeease! She'll be so miserable all on her own. . . ."

Mom and Dad exchanged a look. "Well, I suppose we could ask Helen and Andy what they thought," Dad said, rather reluctantly.

"Yes!" Jasmine flung her arms around his neck. "This is the best Christmas present ever!"

Star sniffed thoughtfully at the pile of bags in the hallway. What was going on? Her owners seemed to be very excited, and kept running up and down the stairs.

"Oh, Star! I almost put that on top of you. Careful, pussycat!" Helen picked her up and petted her. "We're going to miss you. But Jasmine will take care of you so well. We'd better get your things together."

Next door, Jasmine was watching the clock anxiously. "It's almost eight o'clock. Oh, I hope they hurry," she said. "I really want to spend some time with Star before we have to go to school! There's the doorbell!" She leaped up from her chair and rushed to answer it.

Ten minutes later, the Murrays were on their way to the airport, and Jasmine was showing Star where her food and water bowls and litter box were. It was so exciting watching her sniffing around the kitchen, her whiskers twitching delicately as she investigated all the interesting corners. Jasmine picked her up and petted her lovingly, and Star rubbed her ears against Jasmine's cheek.

"Come and see my bedroom," Jasmine told her. She laughed. "You can read my cat books while I'm at school."

"Oh, I thought we'd keep her in the kitchen for now," Mom said.

"But she'd hate that, Mom! It'll be all right. Helen said she's good about using a litter box—she won't make a mess."

Mom frowned. "Are you sure? Won't she be nervous about being in a new place?"

Jasmine looked down at Star, who was purring in her arms. "She doesn't look very nervous. . . ."

Mom nodded, a little reluctantly. "I suppose not. All right. We need to get to school."

Jasmine sighed. "I hope she won't be lonely without me," she murmured.

Star sat in the middle of Jasmine's bed. She was a little confused. She'd been scolded for being in this house before, she remembered. But she was definitely supposed to be here now, because her owners had brought her over that morning, and they'd brought her bowls and her bed, too. Her bed was downstairs in the kitchen, but Jasmine's was nicer.

Star sniffed. The bed smelled like Jasmine, which was comforting. She had stayed in the kitchen for a while, but Jasmine's mom kept watching her and looking worried, and it had made Star feel worried, too. Then Jasmine's mom had gone into another room, and she hadn't liked it when Star tried to play with the wires on her computer. Helen always laughed when she did that.

Star had wondered if she'd done something wrong or if her owners didn't want her anymore, but they hadn't seemed upset. They'd held her and petted her and made a big fuss. Star was quite sure they were coming back. And meanwhile she had Jasmine, who was almost as good. Star stretched out her front paws, yawned, and curled up to sleep. She hoped Jasmine would come home soon.

"Oh, Jasmine, she's adorable! You're so lucky!" Jasmine's friend Lara had come home from school with her to see Star. The girls had gone straight upstairs, and found the kitten snoozing on

Jasmine's bed. She was lying on her back with her paws folded on her soft cream and brown tummy, making a funny little whistling noise—a very small cat's snore.

Lara was whispering, but Star opened one eye thoughtfully, and then bounced up, purring delightedly at Jasmine. She was back!

"Isn't she beautiful?" Jasmine said proudly. Then she sighed. "It's almost like having a cat of my own."

Lara nodded. "Three weeks is a long time. Oh, I wish someone wanted me to cat-sit! I'm sure your parents will get to like her. How can they resist? You never know—then they might let you have your own cat."

Jasmine nodded, sitting down on the bed and hugging Star close. "That's what I'm really hoping, but I'm not sure it'll work. Mom was really griping this morning about not wanting Star to get into her office and mess up her paperwork. She wanted to keep her in the kitchen all day, but I convinced her that it wouldn't be fair. I think they only let me cat-sit Star because they wanted to help out the neighbors. Neither of them are really interested in having pets. They've said I can have a gerbil or a hamster, but I'd much, much rather have a cat."

Lara and Jasmine looked down at Star. She was purring blissfully to herself as Jasmine petted her, in just the right itchy spot down her spine. She looked up at them, then nudged Jasmine's chin lovingly. Lara and Jasmine both sighed. Who wouldn't want such a wonderful cat?

Over the next week, Jasmine wondered if Star had been listening to what she and Lara had said. She seemed to be doing everything she could to charm Jasmine's parents. Maybe it was because Star felt lonely while Jasmine was at school, or maybe it was just that she was a natural people-cat, but she put on her best manners.

On Monday afternoon, Jasmine rushed home from school and let herself in, eager to see Star. But today Star didn't come to say hello. After looking in the kitchen and her bedroom, Jasmine went to her mom's office to see if she knew where the cat was. She put her head around the office door and found Star and her mom, watching the gleams of rainbow light from the glass prism her mom had hanging in the window. Her mom was laughing as Star leaped around the room, chasing the colored flashes on the wall.

"Aren't you supposed to be working?" she asked her mom sternly.

Mom looked guilty. "Yes. But Star came in, and she seemed to want attention. She's so funny, Jasmine—and so athletic. Look at her jumping!"

Star looked up at Jasmine lovingly, and then meowed hopefully at Jasmine's mom.

"Oh, do you want me to swing it for you again, hmm?" Mom reached up to tap the prism, sending the rainbows all around the wall again, and Star was off in a crazy cat dance, leaping and batting at the pretty lights.

Jasmine huffed and went to get

herself a drink. It wasn't that she didn't like her mom getting along with Star—after all, it was exactly what she'd wanted! But Jasmine did feel a tiny bit jealous. *She* played with Star. She and Lara had stopped by the pet shop on the way home, and she'd bought a jingly ball for Star. But Mom's rainbow lights looked much more exciting!

Dad took a little longer to fall for Star. He didn't really spend much time with her, and he got very annoyed when he discovered she'd slept on his favorite sweater and left it covered in brown hairs. But on Sunday morning, Jasmine came downstairs and found Dad reading the newspaper and Star sitting on the kitchen table (which she wasn't allowed to do). She was batting at the back of the paper. Every time she did it, Dad would twitch the paper straight, and Star would wait a few seconds and whack it again with her paw.

Jasmine watched her do it three more times before Dad snorted with laughter and folded up the paper. Star jumped delicately onto his lap and gazed up at him with big green eyes. Jasmine's dad looked down at her as though he wasn't sure quite what he was supposed to do now. He put out a cautious hand and petted her, very lightly down her back. Then he looked up at Jasmine, as if he thought she might tell him he'd done it wrong.

Jasmine sighed and shook her head, smiling. Star had done it again. She'd even managed to win Dad over!

Dad petted Star again, more confidently this time. "This cat," he told Jasmine, as she got herself a bowl of cornflakes, "has got a real sense of humor." He reached over and grabbed a packet of cat treats that had been left on the counter. Star sat up on his lap, her tail twitching eagerly, and he fed her three, one after the other. She crunched them up quickly, with her eyes closed in delight.

"Not too many, Dad." Jasmine pointed at him with her cereal spoon. "She'll get fat. In fact . . ." Jasmine looked worriedly at Star's silky tummy. Was it her imagination, or was it slightly larger than before? "She's starting to get pudgy, Dad, now that I look at her! I bet Mom's been feeding her tons of treats while I'm at school."

Jasmine didn't mention the number of times she'd saved a little bit of chicken or sausage from dinner to feed to Star as an extra-special treat, but she couldn't help feeling a little guilty. She'd just wanted to make Star happy—and it was so sweet the way she nibbled the scraps off her fingers.

Jasmine's mom came downstairs and frowned when Jasmine asked her about the treats. "Well, I gave her one now and then. But not that many, Jasmine. I wouldn't have thought it would be enough to fatten her up." Mom eyed Star thoughtfully as she sat on Dad's lap and washed her ears. "Hmmm. She is looking a bit fatter, you're right. Oh, dear. I don't know much about cats, but

I'm sure it isn't healthy for her to be fat. She could get sick."

"I'll try and get her to run around and play more," Jasmine said, wondering what the Murrays would say if they came home and found they had a fat cat.

Star seemed to be able to tell that Jasmine was worried. She stopped washing and gazed lovingly at her from Dad's lap. Then she sat up on her hind legs with her front paws in the air, as though she was begging to be picked up. It was so funny Jasmine choked on her mouthful of cornflakes.

Dad grinned at her. "You see? She's definitely got a sense of humor!"

Chapter Four

Jasmine started Star's exercise routine the next day when she got home from school. They had decorated their Christmas tree over the weekend, and Star had been fascinated by it. The moment Jasmine and her mom went into the kitchen for a drink, Star had climbed up it and then gotten stuck near the top, wailing frantically as she wobbled on her branch. Jasmine had had to rescue her, and ever since then Star had looked at the tree very suspiciously.

But Star had loved playing with the tinsel, rolling over and over and chewing it. Jasmine wasn't sure how people got cute photos of cats wearing tinsel on their collars. Star would have eaten it before anyone had a chance to get a camera out! So tinsel seemed like a good idea for getting Star to jump around. It was the end of the school term in a couple of days. She could do a lot more exercising with Star when it was winter vacation. She was really looking forward to being at home and being able to play with Star all the time.

Jasmine carefully unwound a bit of silver tinsel from the back of the tree, where no one would really notice it was gone. She crouched down in front of Star, holding the feathery silver tinsel. It shimmered and twinkled, almost as if it were alive, and Star's tail flicked back and forth as she watched it. She dabbed out a paw, and Jasmine twitched the tinsel away, so that Star missed it. The cat sprang forward, paws batting here and there, dancing and springing as Jasmine giggled and waved the tinsel for her. At one point Jasmine was sure that Star leaped at least three feet off the ground in a truly amazing jump.

Eventually Jasmine gave up—she was worn out, though Star was still full of energy. She lay on her back, tugging at the tinsel with her paws and shredding it everywhere.

"Well, that certainly ought to have worked off a few cat treats," Mom said from the doorway, where she'd been watching. "But if you do it again tomorrow, can you use string instead? We won't have any tinsel left at this rate."

Jasmine looked at the silvery pieces all over the floor. "Sorry, Mom. I didn't know she'd tear it up like that. I was going to put it back on the tree."

They looked at each other, and then down at the piece of silver string that was all that was left of the tinsel.

"But maybe not . . ." Jasmine said, giggling, as Star abandoned the tinsel, suddenly tired out, and climbed exhaustedly into her lap. She stretched herself out over Jasmine's legs and went completely floppy, making just a very faint, wheezy purr, as though it was all she had the strength for.

Luckily, the cat dancing game worked almost as well with string, especially when Jasmine invented an excellent new cat toy by tying some of the feathers and felt from a craft set she had onto the string to make it more exciting. They had a great game with it after school on Thursday afternoon. Lara was there, too, to celebrate the start of winter vacation. Mom had gotten them the ingredients to make some snowman cookies, which Jasmine had seen in a magazine, and they sat in the kitchen taking turns licking out the bowl while the cookies baked. Lara offered a teensy bit of mixture to Star, who was sitting next to her on a chair, purring loudly.

Jasmine laughed as Star eagerly licked Lara's fingers. "Don't give her any more. She's such a little pig. Even with all the exercise she's been getting, she's still got that little round tummy. In fact, it seems even bigger now! But I know we're not overfeeding her. I've checked the instructions on the cat food really carefully." She sighed. "I wonder if she's helping herself to food out of another cat's house? I wouldn't put it past her. She's so cute, she can get away with anything."

Lara nodded. "I can't believe she won over your mom and dad, after all you said about them not liking cats."

Jasmine smiled. "It's amazing. I've loved taking care of Star so much, and I'm really going to miss her when the

Murrays get back. I know she'll only be next door, but she won't be sleeping on my bed every night. I've been hoping Star might have charmed Mom and Dad enough that they'd let me get a cat of my own. . . ."

"You really think they will?" said Lara excitedly.

Jasmine reached over and tickled Star lovingly under her chin. "I'm not sure. If the Murrays come home and say Star's gotten fat because we've been overfeeding her, I've got no chance!"

"But I'm sure the Murrays will see how happy Star is and how well you've taken care of her. You really love her, and she adores you—you can tell she does." Lara licked her spoon.

"You wouldn't mind having a cat that wasn't Star, though?"

Jasmine looked thoughtful. "It would be weird," she admitted. "Star's so special. But I know she isn't mine. I've always known that. And you've never seen her with Helen and Andy from next door. She's clearly their cat. I mean, she likes me, but it isn't quite the same." She grinned at Lara. "I need Star number two!"

Jasmine woke up the next morning feeling so happy. At first she couldn't remember why, but then she realized it was the first whole day of winter vacation, and she had a busy day of making Christmas cards and wrapping presents planned. The weather forecast had said there would be a lot of snow today, too. It sounded as though it was going to be a real white Christmas. Jasmine smiled to herself, imagining Star chasing snowflakes, batting at them with her little paws.

She yawned and sat up, ready to pet Star. But she wasn't there. Surprised, Jasmine looked under her covers, in case she had crept underneath. She did that sometimes. No Star. She wasn't hiding in Jasmine's wardrobe, under the bed, or on her beanbag, either.

Jasmine threw on her robe and went downstairs, feeling worried. Star was always there when she woke up! Or sometimes she got sick of waiting and rubbed Jasmine's face until she woke up. But she'd never gone downstairs without Jasmine before.

She found Star in the kitchen, meowing at her mom, who was scooping cat food into her bowl. She didn't even look at Jasmine, just danced and hopped around Mom's legs until she put the bowl down.

"She seems hungry this morning!" Mom commented.

"Mmm." Jasmine didn't want to say anything. She felt a little silly, as if she would be making a fuss about nothing.

But it was the same all day. Star didn't seem to want to play. She ignored the string-and-feathers toy when Jasmine waved it in front of her nose, and she didn't seem interested in wrapping paper at all. She went and slept on the sofa for the whole afternoon, and Jasmine felt really lonely. She'd only been taking care of Star for a couple of weeks, but now that Star didn't want to be with her, it felt awful.

Jasmine watched Star anxiously as she bolted down her dinner. It was the only time Star had been friendly all day—when she wanted Jasmine to feed her.

"She's really starving again," Mom commented, smiling as she watched Star gobbling her food.

Jasmine nodded. "Mom, do you think Star's all right?" she asked worriedly. "She hasn't been very friendly today, not like she usually is. And she slept all afternoon!"

Mom looked at her in surprise. "Well, I don't think she's sick, not the way she's eating!"

Jasmine sighed. "I guess not. Maybe I've been fussing over her too much."

Mom gave her a hug. "Don't worry. Maybe cats have moods just like people. Star might just feel like having some time to herself today."

Star licked all the way round her food bowl and looked at it for a moment in case it magically refilled itself. Then she turned around and walked out of the kitchen, without even looking at Jasmine.

Chapter Five

Star was feeling odd. She didn't know why, but things felt different. She knew she needed to find somewhere quiet and warm, and just curl up and be on her own for a while. But no one seemed to want her to do that!

Star loved Jasmine, and usually she adored all the attention and cuddling she got at Jasmine's house, but not right now. After breakfast that morning, she set off determined to find herself a quiet little nest.

But everywhere in the house seemed busy, and noisy, and full of people— which, considering only Jasmine and her mom were there, was a little strange. Grumpily, Star wandered back into the kitchen to see if there was any more food in her bowl. She was so hungry! Then she spotted the perfect place. . . .

Jasmine's mom had been looking for the red tablecloth she liked to use for Christmas dinner, and she'd left a drawer in the big kitchen cupboard half open. Star peered into it interestedly. It was full of hand towels, dish towels, and tablecloths. Warm, soft, clean things that would be perfect to snuggle up and snooze on. Star wondered why she had never noticed it before—it was just right! She stepped in and curled up at the back of the drawer, yawning and closing her eyes.

Some time later, Star woke up to find herself in complete darkness. She opened her eyes very wide, her heart thudding, unable to think where she was. Then she remembered. Her soft, cozy nest. What had happened to it? Why had it gone dark? She edged forward to where the opening had been and pawed at the wooden walls. She was shut in a tight, dark box! Panicking, Star scratched and scuffled at the front of the drawer, and meowed frantically.

Jasmine and her mom were making cards at the kitchen table. "That sounds like Star," said Jasmine. "I was wondering where she was. She's trapped somewhere, Mom!"

"I don't understand," Jasmine's mom muttered, opening cupboards. "Where can she be? Oh! Oh, dear, the drawer!"

Star blinked and cowered as her nest moved sharply, bumping her head against the top of the drawer. She was pulled out into the light, huddling against the towels.

"Oh, poor Star!" Jasmine lifted her out, and Star snuggled gratefully against her.

"What on earth was she doing in there?" Jasmine's mom asked, sounding a little guilty—she had been the one who had shut Star in the drawer.

"I guess she was just looking for somewhere cozy to sleep," Jasmine suggested. "It wasn't your fault, Mom, you couldn't have known she was there." She stroked Star's head gently. "I know we're cutting back, but I think she really deserves a cat treat!"

Mom and Jasmine went back to card-making, and Star played half-heartedly with some pencils, but she didn't enjoy it very much. She was still feeling the need to find herself a quiet place to rest, and she snuck away to go searching again. This time she found a space under the stairs. It was quiet and dark, and it didn't have a door that anyone could close on her by accident. There were lots of odd things stored under there: boots, roller skates, and a big basket full of gloves and scarves and hats. Star scrambled up the side and turned around several times, purring throatily. This was just right. She would stay here.

But it didn't last. Star was sleeping peacefully when she felt her hiding place shudder as Jasmine raced up the stairs over her head, calling for her. And then Jasmine's mom hauled out the vacuum cleaner, which was right next to her basket bed.

"Oh, Star, I didn't see you. She's down here, Jasmine!" Mom called. And Jasmine came dashing down the stairs again, *thud, thump, thud,* and picked Star up for a cuddle.

Star was still half-asleep, and she was grumpy. She didn't *want* to be picked up. She wanted to be left alone. Angrily, she gave a loud hiss, lashed out with her claws, and scratched Jasmine's arm.

Jasmine was so surprised she yelled and dropped Star, who hissed and shot into the kitchen. There she yowled at Jasmine's mom until she opened the back door.

Jasmine clutched her arm, which was oozing a few spots of blood. She entered the kitchen just in time to see Star's gray and brown striped tail disappearing around the back door. Then she sat down at the kitchen table and cried. Star had scratched her—and then Jasmine had scared her so much by shouting that she'd run away!

Star stayed out in the yard until it got dark, hiding under a clump of bushes.

She was shivering from the cold and knew she couldn't stay out all night. But she'd spent a long time trying to figure out where she could go, and hadn't found anywhere good. Everywhere was too busy, too full of people.

She crept out from under her bush and snuck over to the hole under the fence. She didn't quite have the energy to climb over the fence right now. She dug a little with her claws, widening the hole, then squeezed herself underneath. She had been back to her own yard a fair amount while she was staying at Jasmine's house, trying to make sure all the local cats still knew it was hers. Maybe she could go and make a nest in the bramble patch? She shivered again. No, it was much too cold, colder than she'd ever felt, and the ground was frozen solid. She needed somewhere really warm.

Her house! Of course. She had been back a few times since she'd been staying with Jasmine, to see if the Murrays had come back, but it felt strange and empty. Now the quiet house felt like just what she needed.

Eagerly, Star scurried over to the door and nosed at her cat flap, squeezing herself in.

It was so quiet. No one around. And warm, or at least warmer than the bramble bushes. Perfect. She looked around the kitchen thoughtfully, trying to think of a good place to go.

After her experience with drawers at Jasmine's house, she didn't want anywhere too small and tight. Star set off upstairs and tried all the beds, but they weren't right, either—too out in the open. At last, she found the linen closet. The door was shut, but it only had a light catch, and the door itself was made of wooden slats that were perfect for claws to hook between.

Star pulled it open and crept in, sniffing delightedly at the clean, fresh smell. On the floor was a pile of old towels, and she curled up on them, closing her eyes peacefully. She was home. Just in time.

Chapter Six

It was almost bedtime. By now Jasmine was panicking. She couldn't find Star anywhere. She'd even checked the kitchen cupboard drawer, just in case.

"She ran away because I shouted at her!" Jasmine wailed. "It's all my fault!"

"She's probably just out exploring," Jasmine's mom suggested, trying to calm her down. "You know she likes to go off and sniff around in those brambles next door."

Jasmine bolted out into the dark yard, without even putting on her coat, and raced down to the end. She climbed up on her mom's rock garden—which she definitely wasn't allowed to do—and peered over at the bramble patch at the end of the Murrays' yard. A few tiny snowflakes drifted gently past her nose, and she shivered.

"Star! Star! Here, kitty, kitty . . ." She tried again and again, but no little striped cat appeared out of the trailing branches, looking up at her lovingly.

Jasmine wandered sadly back across the yard. She looked so unhappy that her mom didn't bother scolding her for not wearing a coat.

"She isn't there."

"You don't know that, Jasmine. She might just not want to come out."

"But why?" Jasmine cried. "Why doesn't she want to play anymore? What have I done to make her not like me? I was supposed to be taking care of her! She used to like me, I know she did, but then she scratched me! She's never done that before."

She slumped down in a kitchen chair, and her mom sat down next to her. "Jasmine, it isn't your fault. You've taken great care of her. Cats are like that sometimes. They can get touchy and grumpy, just like people can. She's probably stalking blackbirds in a yard a few doors down. I'm sure she'll be back soon."

Jasmine gave her a disbelieving look. "It's starting to snow out there, Mom! It's freezing! Star wouldn't want to stay out in this weather—she likes being warm." Jasmine looked over at Star's bowl, which was full of food. "She hasn't even come back for her dinner, and she must be really hungry by now. Oh, what if she doesn't come back? What are we going to do? How will we tell Andy and Helen?"

Mom thought for a moment, then smiled. "Do you know what, I bet Star's probably gone back home!"

Jasmine's mouth opened, then she grinned back at her mom. "Of course she has!" She hugged her around the waist lovingly. "Oh, Mom, you're so smart. Why didn't I think of that?"

The house felt strange—somewhat cold and very quiet. Jasmine couldn't help feeling guilty, as though she was trespassing. She was glad Mom had come with her.

She had hoped that Star would come out to meet her as soon as she opened the door, but no little striped cat appeared, meowing in welcome. Then Jasmine had an awful thought—what if Star had accidentally gotten shut inside somewhere like she had earlier? That was only because Mom had shut the drawer, of course, but Star could easily have gotten herself trapped if a door had swung closed. And no one had been here to let her out! Jasmine ran through the house, calling and calling for Star, until her voice hurt and Mom told her gently to stop.

Tucked away inside the warm linen closet, Star could hear Jasmine calling her name. She was tempted to meow and let Jasmine know where she was—she missed her soft petting, the loving whispers, and the delicious treats Jasmine always had for her. But for now she needed to be alone. She wasn't ready quite yet. Soon.

Mom had her arm around Jasmine as they walked back home. "She'll turn up," she told her, trying to sound encouraging. "You know Helen said she'd been wandering around a lot."

"Did you find her?" Dad opened the front door as they came down the path.

Jasmine shook her head sadly, and Dad gave her a hug. "I'll help you look for her tomorrow," he promised. But he gave his wife a worried frown over Jasmine's head.

"I don't think we'll ever find her!" Jasmine wailed.

"Oh, sweetie, you're getting way ahead of yourself! If she isn't back in the morning, then we'll go and look for her. But she will be. You'll see."

Just before Jasmine went to bed that night, she went to her window and peered out at the night-filled yard. There were deep shadows everywhere and it looked frightening. Jasmine hated to think of Star out there somewhere all on her own. Last time Star had been out at night,

Jasmine had rescued her. But now she wasn't even sure Star would want to be rescued. Or at least not by her.

"If only I hadn't shouted at her like that," she whispered miserably to her reflection in the window.

Suddenly, the dark sky filled with thick snowflakes, and Jasmine watched sadly as they began to cover the yard in frozen whiteness.

Chapter Seven

We're having a wonderful time. I saw a newspaper and can't believe it's snowing back at home, when we're sunbathing and swimming in the ocean here! Hope you're really enjoying it, though—it's the first time Star has seen snow. Make a snowman for us!
Love,
Helen and Andy
PS: Merry Christmas! Go next door and look in the cupboard under the sink to find a little present for you and one for Star, her favorite salmon treats!

A fat tear splashed onto the keyboard. It was snowing still, just in time to be a white Christmas, the first one in years. Everyone was really excited about it, but Jasmine couldn't care less. Lara had invited her to build a snowman in her yard, but Jasmine couldn't face it. She just kept imagining poor Star, shivering in the middle of a snowstorm, ice dripping off her whiskers. It was the worst Christmas ever. She couldn't even feel excited about presents.

"Do you think we should call and tell them she's gone?" Jasmine asked her mom sadly. The Murrays' e-mail said they'd gotten her a present to say thank you for taking care of Star so well. . . . She felt so miserably guilty.

"They left the number of their hotel, didn't they?"

"Yes, they did," said Mom. "But Star's only been gone one night, and we don't want to ruin their vacation. There's nothing they could do. I'm sure she'll be back by the time they fly home in a few days, anyway."

Jasmine nodded. She supposed Mom was right. It would only make the Murrays really sad, and there was a chance she might still find her. . . .

She'd spent the morning going up and down the street with Dad, peering under bushes and looking behind fences. Jasmine had even asked everyone she knew in the street to look in their sheds and garages, and to ask their neighbors to do so also. Feeling helpless, she went to put on her coat. She didn't really think she'd find Star now, but she couldn't give up. It was Christmas Eve tomorrow. How could she leave Star lost out in the snow on Christmas?

"Are you going out again?" her mom asked worriedly. "Honestly, Jasmine, you'll freeze! Do you want me to come?"

Jasmine shook her head. "It's okay. Maybe later."

She was plodding up the sidewalk through the snow, which was already turning gray and slushy, when she had a thought. The Murrays' e-mail had said they'd left some of Star's favorite salmon cat treats, and Jasmine knew she really did love those. She turned into the most adoring little cat ever when you were about to open a packet—weaving through your legs, meowing loudly. Perhaps if Star was hiding out in one of the yards somewhere—and that was what Jasmine was hoping—she'd come back if she smelled those yummy salmon treats.

Jasmine dashed back home to get the Murrays' keys, and scuttled down the path to their house.

Of course, she shouldn't be opening Star's present before Christmas, Jasmine thought to herself as she ripped open the shiny wrapping paper, but this was an emergency.

She was just tearing at the foil pouch with her nails when she heard it. A loud piercing, demanding, very squeaky meow. From upstairs.

Star was here!

Although that didn't sound quite like Star. Could another cat have gotten in?

Jasmine crept up the stairs, feeling half-hopeful, half-scared. She wasn't quite sure what to expect—even if it was Star up there, would she be happy to see her? She'd been so grumpy the day she disappeared.

The strange meowing continued as Jasmine reached the landing. She opened one of the bedroom doors and peered around. It seemed empty. But then the squeaky meow came again, and she realized that there was a door down the hall that she hadn't noticed. And it was very slightly open.

"Star?" Jasmine whispered nervously.

There was a moment's silence, and then Jasmine heard a very familiar purr. Star! It was definitely her, and she was purring in welcome. Jasmine wanted to race over and hug her, but she told herself to be calm and not get too excited. Her enthusiasm was probably what had made Star leave in the first place. She walked quietly over to the linen closet and very gently opened the door.

There was Star, lying curled on a pile of towels and purring delightedly at Jasmine.

And snuggled up next to her were two tiny newborn kittens.

Chapter Eight

Star stared up at Jasmine, purring proudly. She was very pleased that Jasmine had found her—she wanted to show off her beautiful babies. And she was absolutely starving—she hadn't eaten for a whole day now, and she'd been feeding her kittens, too. She had thought about going to find Jasmine, and some food, but she hadn't wanted to leave her kittens—she knew they needed her. She had hoped and hoped that Jasmine would come, and now she had. She meowed at Jasmine, who seemed to be holding a food packet.

Jasmine crouched down and poured some salmon treats out into her hand. "Oh, you must be starved, poor Star," she murmured as she gently scattered them in front of Star's nose, without getting too close to the kittens. She didn't want to upset Star. Luckily, Star didn't seem to mind being found, but Jasmine knew she would be very protective of her little ones. She sat back on her heels, a little way away from the closet, and laughed to herself. "I thought I'd been feeding you too much, Star! I thought you were just getting pudgy, but you were going to have kittens!"

Star licked her kittens' heads fondly with her own little pink tongue. Jasmine's eyes filled with tears. It was so grown up, such a mother cat thing to do, and Star was only a baby herself, really too young to have kittens.

"But I guess you didn't know you were too young," Jasmine murmured. "Wow. Andy and Helen have three cats now—they're so lucky!" She looked admiringly at the kittens. They were about as long as two of her fingers. One of them was a gorgeous striped orange color, and the other looked like a tiny baby Star, only with slightly more gray in her tabby fur. Their eyes were closed, and their ears were almost invisible, still tucked against their heads.

Star gave her a slightly anxious look, and Jasmine smiled. "They're beautiful. Beautiful kittens." She couldn't tell if they were boys or girls. Then she frowned slightly. She hoped Star was okay. Was there anything she should do for her? Did she need to go to a vet?

Jasmine carefully backed away from the closet, not wanting to startle Star or the kittens—although they were fast asleep and didn't look like much could disturb them right now. "I'll be back soon," she murmured. "And I'll bring you some more food and water, and—and a litter box."

Jasmine raced downstairs and back to her own house. "Mom! Mom!" she called excitedly.

Her mom rushed out of the kitchen. "Did you find her? Oh, you did, didn't you? Well done, Jasmine!" She peered over Jasmine's shoulder, expecting to see Star following her. "But where is she?"

Jasmine beamed and hugged her. She'd almost forgotten how miserable and frightened she had been about losing Star, and now an incredible relief flooded over her in waves. She needed to hold on to someone. "You're not going to believe it," she said into her mom's shoulder.

"What? Has she been somewhere really obvious all the time? Where is she?"

"She's in the linen closet next door." Jasmine grinned at her. "And she had kittens!"

"No!" Jasmine's mom gasped. "You mean it? Star did? How could we not have noticed she was pregnant?"

Jasmine laughed. "I don't know! I guess we just thought she was too young. There are only two kittens, so I think that's why she wasn't really that big. We did think she was fat, didn't we? I need to go and find all my cat books, Mom—I need to know what we should do!"

Jasmine was very careful not to upset Star by fussing over her and the kittens too much. She knew now that Star had been grumpy because she was about to have the kittens, and her cat instincts were telling her she needed to hide away somewhere safe. But she was pretty sure that Star would still be touchy about anyone coming too close. So she left kitten food—her books said that was what Star needed right now, since it was high in energy—and water bowls and a litter box just outside the closet. She then strictly rationed herself to a five-minute visit every couple of hours. Her mom had called the vet whose number the Murrays had left. The receptionist had said that it sounded like Star was doing great all by herself, but to call if there were any problems, and the vet would come out and see her.

It had gone from being the worst Christmas Jasmine could have imagined to the absolute best. She spent the time between her visits to Star and the kittens looking up kitten care on the computer and biting her nails, wishing the time would go faster.

"I wish we could go pet the kittens," she said to her mom the next morning. "I know we shouldn't, because they're too young, but they look so soft and cuddly."

"Mmm." Jasmine's mom wasn't really listening, since she was trying to figure out exactly how long she had to cook the Christmas turkey the next day. "Do you think we should have parsnips, Jasmine? I can't remember if you like them."

"I don't," Jasmine said. "Ooh, Mom, we'll have to take Star some Christmas dinner tomorrow. Just a little bit. Please?"

Mom shook her head, laughing. "Poor Helen and Andy, coming home to find a cat eating Christmas dinner in their linen closet!"

Jasmine smiled. "They won't mind,"

she said. She knew how much the Murrays adored Star. "They'll be so excited about the kittens. It's going to be such a great surprise. They're so lucky, coming back to three cats instead of one!"

Mom looked thoughtful. "I don't know. Three cats is a lot, all at once. But I'm sure they'll be able to find good homes for the kittens."

Jasmine blinked back sudden tears. She hadn't thought that the Murrays might not keep the kittens—she'd been really looking forward to having three cats next door now! She didn't notice that Mom was watching her, a strange, thoughtful expression on her face.

"I'll just go and check on them all," Jasmine muttered. "I'll take Star some more of that special cat milk." Mom had made an emergency trip to the pet store yesterday to buy some kitten food and some milk that was made to be safe for cats' stomachs.

She sat by the linen closet door watching Star, who was looking down at her feeding babies with a very contented look on her face.

"Oh, Star, I hope the Murrays will keep them," Jasmine murmured. "I don't want you to lose your kittens!"

But Star wasn't listening. She was gently licking the orange-colored kitten's ears, as if making sure they were perfectly clean was the most important thing in the world.

Jasmine woke up early on Christmas morning. She smiled delightedly as she felt the heavy weight of her stocking next to her feet and sat up to see if she could feel what was in it.

Then she frowned. Was that meowing? Jasmine turned on her bedside light and listened again. Star was safe next door, and she'd checked on her right before bed the night before, but—yes, there it was again. Jasmine ran downstairs and unlocked the back door to find Star standing there, with the little tabby kitten held in her mouth. Star dashed inside—she was probably worried about the kitten catching cold, Jasmine thought, looking out at the yard as she closed the door. There had been another snowfall in the night, and the grass was covered in a fresh white layer, which looked weird and blue-gray in the darkness.

"Where are you going, Star?" she asked, following the little cat as she trotted through the dark hallway. She flinched as Star started to climb the stairs, determinedly heaving the kitten up each step. Jasmine desperately wanted to help but wasn't sure if Star would let her.

Eventually, they reached the landing, and Star made for Jasmine's bedroom, where she stared meaningfully at the wardrobe.

"Oh!" Jasmine laughed. "You want to have your bed in my wardrobe?" she asked delightedly. She opened the door at once and quickly pulled out her sneakers, then fluffed an old fleece blanket into a comfy nest for Star and the kittens.

Star scrambled in and dropped the kitten gently on the blanket, where it wriggled and made a faint, squeaky little meow. Then Star trotted off to go get the other kitten.

By lunchtime, Star was well settled, with her food bowls next to the wardrobe. Mom had brought her little extra morsels of turkey, and Jasmine had even hung some tinsel over the wardrobe door, to make it look Christmasy.

Jasmine had wondered if she might have to go and sleep on the sofa, but Star didn't seem to mind her being there— and so Jasmine was able to watch her and the kittens a lot more. They were so cute. She was sure that the little tabby one was going to open its eyes soon. They were both adorable, of course, but the tabby baby was so much like Star, Jasmine couldn't help loving it most of all. She was almost sure it was a girl kitten, since it looked so like its mom.

It was a different sort of Christmas Day, but peeping in at the sleeping kittens, Jasmine thought it was the nicest she'd ever had.

118

Two days later, the Murrays arrived home. They hurried next door to Jasmine's house as soon as they'd dropped off their bags.

Jasmine answered the door, hugging her secret to herself and trying not to giggle.

"Come and see!" she told them.

"Is Star asleep on your bed?" Helen asked, as they followed Jasmine upstairs.

"Not exactly," Jasmine said to them mysteriously. She led them into her room and stood back so they could see the scene in her wardrobe.

Star seemed to know she had visitors. She was posed like a queen, and Jasmine was sure she was eyeing the kittens anxiously to make sure they were looking beautiful, too.

"Goodness!" Helen crouched down to look. "I had no idea she was pregnant!"

"Neither did we," Jasmine explained. "She started behaving strangely, and then she disappeared. . . . We did wonder if it was because she was really missing you. But actually she was having babies in your linen closet! Mom cleaned it up," she added.

"Smart little Star . . ." Helen murmured, and Andy shook his head in amazement. "Talk about keeping it quiet. So now we've got three cats!"

"You're so lucky," Jasmine sighed, and Helen looked at her thoughtfully. Leaving Jasmine to tell Andy the whole story right from the beginning, she beckoned Jasmine's mom out of the room.

They came back a couple of minutes later, just as Jasmine was describing

Star arriving at the back door on Christmas morning.

"Your mom's agreed that we'd better let them all stay here for the moment. Star probably won't want to be moved," Helen said. "As long as you don't mind sharing your bedroom, that is?"

"Of course not!" said Jasmine. "What will you do when the kittens are bigger?" she asked. "Will you keep them all?" She wasn't sure that she wanted to know the answer.

"Well, three cats is kind of a lot. . . ." Helen said, smiling at Jasmine's mom. "I really love the little orange-colored one—I have a feeling he takes after Tiger, that handsome orange cat down the road."

Jasmine gulped. They didn't want the tabby kitten! She couldn't bear the idea of her special little Christmas kitten being unwanted. It was so unfair.

She almost didn't hear Helen as she went on, "But I have an idea. A way that the tabby kitten could have her own home and stay close to her mom."

Jasmine looked up, her eyes full of hope. "You mean . . ."

Helen grinned at her. "Why not?"

Jasmine looked over at her parents. There was no way Mom and Dad would let her. Was there?

Mom smiled. "Would you like to keep her, Jasmine? You know your dad and I have never been crazy about having a cat, but Star won me over. She's so sweet. Your dad really took to having a cat as well—he was so upset when Star was missing. I'd been wondering whether we could keep one of the kittens even before Helen asked me," Mom went on. "You looked after Star so well. Dad and I were really proud of you."

"And as the kitten practically started her life in your wardrobe, I don't really think we could say no!" Dad laughed.

Jasmine looked down at the little silvery kitten with new eyes. She could be hers! Star gazed at her lovingly, as though she approved of the idea, too.

"What will you name her, Jasmine?" Mom asked.

Jasmine thought for a moment. Something Christmasy. Then she smiled, remembering Star's favorite toy. "Tinsel," she said, reaching out, very gently, to pet her new cat.

Also available:

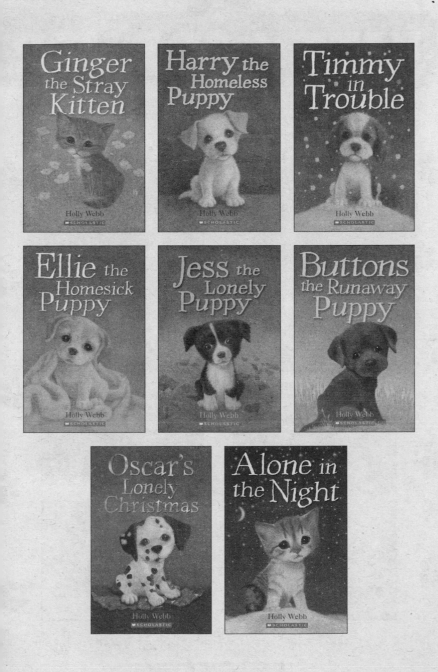

KITTY CORNER

Where kitties get the love they need

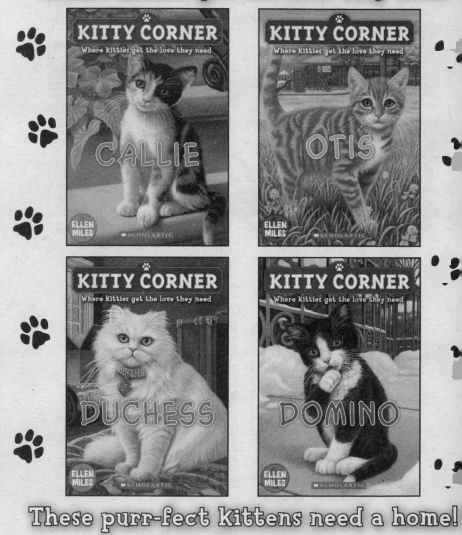

These purr-fect kittens need a home!